Stories From a Fledgling Writer

Also by Blaire Sawusch:

Vestiges

Stories From a Fledgling Writer

BLAIRE SAWUSCH

Stories From a Fledgling Writer

The following are entirely works of fiction. Take them as you will.

Copyright © 2019 by Blaire Sawusch.

Published in the United States by Blaire Sawusch in 2019.

All rights reserved. No parts of this book may be reproduced – except for brief excerpt properly cited – without the written permission of the author.

ISBN: 9781077768239

blairephoenyxpyre.wordpress.com

@phoenyxpyre

*For my mother and my aunt Marilynn.
Thank you for always supporting my writing and
being the best unpaid editors in the world.*

Table of Contents

Silence in the City 1

The Note 26

Character Sketch: Missing 36

The Last Plant 41

More Than a $20 Memory 52

Path of the Unforgotten 59

Vision of the Void 64

Minisaga: *The Tree* 82

Shady Vale 83

Essay: The Reclaiming of North America 101

Fire 109

The Darkest Places of the Earth 128

Stories From a

Fledgling Writer

Silence in the City

She walked with exceptional poise, the grace of a lioness about to pounce. Her three-inch heels tapped the pavement, seemingly syncopated with his heartbeat. The early morning Chicago lights illuminated the car windshields as her long jacket trailed helplessly behind her, her upright posture demanding the cars stop before her.

And they did. They always did.

Anthony had worked with her for five years now, two of which were after their small booming company was offered a place in a big office building in central Chicago. It was called *The Peak*, and rightfully so. It was the tallest building in the nation, one of the new architectural improvements of the decade, allowing not only more floors, but also complete energy efficiency. It also held the nation's leading medical researchers, from raw technology to sophisticated procedures. Their division specialized in disease prevention research, focusing on biological warfare.

Stephanie was incredibly intelligent, young, and, to Anthony, exceptionally beautiful. He admired her ability to handle the company with ease, always on her toes and never late for anything. She was a morning person, and the way she briskly jogged across the street – without coffee in hand – let him know right away that she was not as early as she wanted to be.

He had never once seen her in the morning on her way to work but he was glad he had, even if it was just this once. If the world were to end tomorrow, the vision of her dashing across the road would be the last thing he would want to remember. Her shoulders square, her head held high…and how did she walk in those shoes? The biggest mystery of the world: women walking on stilts. How did they do it? And her…

He quickly dodged the oncoming taxicab and retreated back to the curb. He had forgotten he had stepped out to cross. Surely, if he were to try and cross the street as she did, they would run him over.

Incredible.

Anthony looked up at the sky and smiled at the puffy white clouds, checked both ways, and crossed in the clearing. He took a sip of his cappuccino as his mind drifted back to her. He realized then he could do something nice for her, in her rush, she had forgotten her own fuel, as she called it. If he had any hope of getting her attention past just being business colleagues, he had to start somewhere.

The coffee shops were already crammed full of people coming off the packed sidewalks and streets of the early morning traffic. Taxis zipped by as he opened the door to the Starbucks. The walls were lined with pictures of the old days, antique pictures of the "L" in its prime, and airplanes that needed several engines to leave the ground. The Holovision hanging in the corner displayed the news with a reporter wrapped in a fur jacket.

Anthony quickly made his way through the line and ordered her the usual, a caramel mocha, and rushed two blocks down to the office.

The building was bustling in the early AM. Businessmen and women crammed into stainless steel elevators trying to make their mark on the world. If only it was as easy as leaving fingerprints on the silver elevator buttons. Seconds later the musical voice of the elevator announced *floor four hundred and thirty*, and a dozen people flooded out into the main lobby. Anthony kept to himself as he stepped through the surge of people onto his hallway, walking past the black, disk-thin printers and copiers. He finally reached his desk. She smiled up at him, her bright eyes like the millions of volts of electricity that pulsed through *The Peak* daily.

"I brought you a coffee, Stephanie," he ventured, trying to seem confident as he set it down on her desk.

She looked surprised, and then relieved, "Oh, thank you. You didn't have to do that!" She took it without missing a beat. Her eyes widened with joy as she nodded. "Fuel for the human mind," she laughed.

He grinned and sat down to do his work. He wasn't focused long before Stephanie grabbed his attention and handed him the morning report in her Holopad.

"They say there are gangs in the alleyways administering a new drug that renders the victim mindless. What do you think of that?" she asked, concern creeping into her every word. He held the device up and read what little information that had been released from the shimmering screen. It was mostly information leaked to the press about two homeless men who had been given the drug and were admitted to the hospital.

"It says down at the bottom that the authorities will have it under control soon. It's probably just a short-term drug, and nothing to be worried about. Just a couple of teenagers trying to be funny," he handed her back the Holopad as she nodded.

"That's kind of what I thought, too. I asked a couple others this morning already, and everyone seems to have similar thoughts…" she trailed off, as though unsure of her beliefs.

"You seem fairly concerned about it," he said after a moment, "I'm sure it will be under control by tomorrow."

"Yes, I suppose you're right," she sighed.

Not long after finishing a report, their secretary, Oscar, came over hurriedly, flipping the information from his Holopad up onto her computer screen with a flick of his finger. "Why aren't we involved in this at all?" he questioned her, looking worried and angry.

"They'll call if they need us, Oscar," she said quietly, "the government knows we're here. We don't typically do field work, and any pertinent information we would have has already been published. We might get some calls about clarifications, but that will probably be it," she smiled reassuringly at him, but he walked away muttering with the frame of the Holopad clamped in his hand.

"What did it say?" Anthony asked, watching Oscar wander for a moment and then return to his desk.

"The press seems angry about the lack of information being reported, and several people are also speaking out about the public's right to know if they are safe," she said quietly. "It seems that more people have recently been admitted to the hospital, and no one knows if they are getting better, or even what this drug is that they were given, or how and by whom."

"How long ago was that article released?"

"Just three minutes ago," she replied, looking at him as if searching for answers. Answers she knew he didn't have, but she looked anyway. If anyone could find the answers, it was her, he thought, not him. *Are we safe?* her intelligent brown eyes seemed to ask.

"If you'd like, I can walk you home tonight. Maybe we can grab a bite to eat and talk about it some more. It seems as if you have more to say about what's going on," he offered.

"I would really appreciate that," she said, concern still furrowed in her brow, but now a smile came upon her face, and he could feel the lightness in his feet as he pushed his chair back to his desk.

The day went by quickly for Anthony. Between a constant flow of projects and meetings, he hardly checked the time. Before he knew it, it was 5 PM. The antique clock tower in the distance chimed, and he looked over to see Stephanie putting things away and packing up.

"Do you still want to go?" he asked.

"Of course!"

"Alright then, where's your favorite place?" he said, swinging his bag over his shoulder.

"Have you ever been to *Indigo*?" she asked, "It's a really nice place, just a block from here."

"I've actually never heard of it. How long has it been there?" he pushed the down button for the elevator, and a soft *ding* followed.

"It's been there for a couple of years now. They have all sorts of experimental beer. My sister really likes their basil lager." she laughed.

"I'm more of a wine person, myself," Anthony replied, watching as the floor numbers flashed by as they descended.

"They have an excellent wine selection too," she assured him.

"Sounds great," he smiled, looking at her as she returned the grin.

The lobby of *The Peak* was nearly cleared out, only a few people stood talking over the seal in its center, and the usual security guards wandered throughout and stood by the doors. This was the latest he had stayed at work in quite a while, but he was still surprised to see how vacant the building now was. People would sometimes stay for hours talking after they got out of work, mostly visiting with friends, or catching up with people they knew from other divisions.

Stephanie didn't say a word, but out of the corner of his eye he could see her purse her lips, probably harboring the same concern and wonder. They made their way down to *Indigo* mostly in silence, using some small talk to carry the conversation.

When they arrived, they found the restaurant not too busy, and were seated immediately.

"Isn't this place usually busy on Thursday nights?" Stephanie asked the hostess.

"Normally, yes. It's been surprisingly quiet all day. I think it's because of what the newspapers are saying and all, about that underground drug. It's been making everyone rather nervous," she smiled politely, but Anthony could see the worry in her eyes. "Your server will be with you shortly," she said, and then turned away quickly.

People were skittish in a big city, but perhaps they had a right to be.

Stephanie picked up her menu and looked for a while before setting it down again. She looked at Anthony, and they seemed to exchange a mutual feeling of fear and worry. He wondered what the other areas of Chicago were like, and just how far out the news had spread. He wished he could do something to comfort her… or even himself. Anthony could sense the situation beginning to bother him more and more as the day progressed, and now it had come to its peak when people went home early and, in a rush, not congregating at restaurants and pubs along the way as they usually did.

"How serious do you think the situation really is?" he asked after a moment.

"Hospitals are not allowed to release anything, and the press can't get their hands on any kind of information. It's the lack of information, I think, that is scaring people. Depending on what kind of long-term effect this drug has, I think it could become very serious, very fast," she replied, keeping her voice low.

"Do you think it's a terrorist act?" he whispered.

She shook her head and looked off out the window. "I just don't know, Anthony. It could be anything. You would think we would be quick to blame if they thought it was coming from another country, or there would be something about investigating the source. So far, there seems to be nothing. I think Oscar is right. It's odd that we haven't been contacted at all, as the leading company in research and medical development made *exactly* for this kind of event. I would do it myself, if I could," she trailed off as the server came over to introduce herself.

Dinner arrived quickly, with the lack of people service was much faster than Stephanie said she had ever experienced it. They paid the tab and left the comfort of the restaurant and headed back into the city. The sun had gone down completely now, and floating streetlights illuminated their way. Stephanie lived a short distance from *The Peak*, only four blocks, in a nice apartment complex. He walked her back without an incident, and then turned for home himself.

The next morning, he awoke as usual. But when he arrived at the office, Stephanie's desk was exactly the same as she had left it the night before. An hour passed and still nothing changed. He began to worry she never made it to work that morning. He called her phone, and it went to voicemail. He opened his desk drawer to write himself a reminder on a sticky note and found an envelope with his name written on the front of it.

Anthony looked around to make sure no one was watching. He quickly opened it, recognizing her handwriting, and began reading.

So, they did end up contacting us, he thought, pausing for a moment to let the information sink in before putting the letter safely in his bag. He was right; he knew that if anyone could figure it out it was her. The government had contacted her early that morning, and she was working with them to find out more about the drug. Her letter warned that it was incredibly top secret, and only him and Oscar were to know where she was.

He considered shredding the letter for a moment when the phone rang.

"Hello?"

"Anthony!" a voice whispered.

"Stephanie! Is everything alright?"

"I'm fine, but Chicago isn't, and you won't be either if you don't leave right away. Catch the next fastest ride out of there. If you don't get out by tonight, they will lock you in there!"

"What are you talking about? What's going on?" he whispered frantically.

"I'm so sorry Anthony, but we are working hard to figure this drug out. I can't tell you much, and I made an effort to find a secure line. If they find out I've told you anything they might come looking for you," she breathed, "but I can tell you that it doesn't look good. Some group of young teens accidentally developed a highly complex drug that's administered just by a pin, and it completely shuts down some of the major functioning in the brain, making its victim basically mindless. We caught some of them, and they admitted to doing it as a joke, thinking it was a game to see how many people who weren't paying attention they could get."

"That's insane," he replied.

"It gets worse," she continued, "it's so complex that when the drug is first introduced, it makes the person unaware, or ignore the fact that something might be wrong with them. Then it's too late, and they're gone. I'm sorry Anthony, I have to go. It's much more serious than you think, I can't even tell you all the information," she whispered.

"Wait!" he cried.

"Goodbye," she said quickly, and then the line went dead.

He quickly packed his things and went downstairs. At the curb he called a taxi and told the driver to take him northwest toward the airport. Traffic was a mess, and an hour went by before he first saw the barriers. *It's too late,* he thought, as an armed guard turned away car after car, telling them not to worry, and the quarantine was only a safety precaution.

"It will most likely clear up by Monday," the guard said to the cab driver.

The mini Holovision in the cab displayed that all flights going into and out of Chicago were delayed until further notice. Reporters showed images of road barriers that stretched for miles around the city.

Anthony tipped the driver well after arriving back at his apartment, and immediately called Stephanie. He was again sent to voicemail.

He paced back and forth in his kitchen, beginning to think about how much food he had, and whether it was safe to go out and stockpile more.

Night came and he still hadn't left. Anthony sat in the small living room looking out the window, watching the cars on the road. His phone rang then, and he picked up.

"Did you get out?" she asked.

"No," he said softly, "It was too late. They already set up the barricades."

"I'm so sorry."

"It's not your fault. How is the research coming?"

"You don't understand," she said, dread creeping into her voice, "we managed to catch the culprits before they could do more damage. Thankfully they were willing to cooperate, but…"

"But what?" he prodded.

"But the drug leaked into the water supply."

***

He saw her again in his memory, dashing across the street late for work the day before everything changed. He saw the cabs stop, and the bright morning lights reflect off her glossy shoes – the city all around her like a protector. Now, Chicago was empty. Completely cut off and quarantined. Walls were quickly built and put up. One day he saw planes fly overhead carrying large concrete barriers. He wondered if any of the drug had gone beyond the city into the country.

Before he stopped leaving his apartment, he watched as the city slowly worsened. Streetlights were tipped over in protest, marchers breaking store windows and everything not of significant value as they went. But soon, the protesting stopped, and the few left to their senses began to raid empty houses and buildings for food and water. He could still see a giant poster board that read "Free Chicago" from his window laying on the streets below.

Although he was trapped, it was comforting to him that Stephanie had gotten out before all of this. He wondered if she knew he was still alive. He wondered what she was doing, if she was okay, if she went to work somewhere in Washington, early every morning. He wondered if the cars still stopped for her in the streets. He wondered if anyone drove cars anymore.

He lost all contact with her about a week ago when the power suddenly shut off. They had been communicating by phone, using as little information as possible in order to lessen the chances of her being caught. After the drug seeped into the city water, thousands of people were affected. He remembered telling everyone in his apartment to not drink the water, but some were not as careful as others.

Anthony rose from his chair and opened his bag for the first time since he left work three weeks ago. He dumped everything out onto the table in front of him. There was nothing new or helpful there for him. He saw her letter, and reread it, reminded again how quickly things changed. He remembered thinking that maybe they were going to let the city go, let it all work itself out once they realized it was hopeless. People had tried breaking through the barricades, but to no avail. Now, there weren't enough people left to make a substantial force against them.

Most of the people affected by the drug were found and brought to the hospitals. There, they slept in beds, awaiting whatever miracle people believed would come. People were frightened beyond belief, but now most of those who remained healthy came to help and take care of those who were not.

He got up and walked into his kitchen, taking out some of his provisions and leaning against the fridge that had long since stopped running. He looked out the large window of his apartment, still expecting to see the cars and people walking below, waiting for the flashing signs and electronic advertisements to flick on again, as if nothing had happened.

He believed his eyes had cheated him when he saw a small light in the distance, something he knew hadn't been there since the city went dark.

He blinked, looked over at the candle he had fashioned to see if it was that. The flame was steady. He looked out again and saw the light once more, noticing now that it was pulsating.

He stood for a moment, then grabbed his jacket and headed out the door. He hesitated at the foot of his apartment, and then wrenched open the door. He was first struck by the smell, and then crippling fear. He shut the door quickly. Taking a deep breath to steady himself, he reopened it, and walked out.

The city looked as if it had shriveled up. Any sort of life had extinguished long ago. The light caught his eye again, and he quickened his pace. He realized it could be some kind of trick, some kind of malicious intent to draw in those who still believed in miracles. He didn't care, he realized. He wasn't doing any good sitting in his apartment.

He hadn't even visited the hospital to help, only hearing about it from others on his floor who went.

He drew closer, and realized it was an old clothing store. The window on the door had been shattered, and mannequins that once presumably modeled clothing were tipped over. Taking in the scene, he ducked through the entryway, and took out a flashlight. There wasn't as much dust as he thought there would be, and everything was relatively still ordered. The shelves were bare, and the cash register tipped over on the floor with the money tray opened. He continued to walk farther in and saw again the light. It was coming from the back of the store, behind a wooden door that had seen better days. The light slipped out from the multiple holes surrounding where the doorknob used to be. A mouse scurried out from a well warn path underneath the door. Anthon held his breath and opened the door.

Beakers and test tubes were strewn about the counter, and a laptop sat amongst them, a ball of light gliding back and forth across the screen, signaling sleep mode. Whoever's it was, they had just left, he thought. He walked in slowly and tapped the screen with his finger. The machine came back to life, revealing a program pulled up that he recognized right away. In the top right corner, the name *Stephanie Burrow* was displayed. Anthony felt his heart jump, and throb in his ears. The page was scrolled all the way to the end, and the words "antidote complete" were flashing at the bottom.

The Note

"You're just yanking my chain," his mother laughed. She had been listening to his wild story from the start. He was seven years old at the time, and he loved to embellish real life events. At first the tale started off as a believable story, only little white lies where he couldn't remember clearly what had happened at school that day. Then, they expanded into epic stories that could have been straight out of Homer's *Odyssey*; where sea serpents came alive beneath the swing sets and giants lived in the forest next to the school.

"I swear it was real! We were all sitting in class like any normal day. And like any normal day, a huge giant came… right out in the – out in the woods! We all told the teacher to look. We told her to look and she did," he paused, bouncing in his seat with excitement, "she said we needed to focus more," he concluded somberly. His small, round sad face brightened again as he threw his hands into the air like his father did when he told bedtime stories. "Then-then at recess - mom, are you paying attention? Mom! – at recess we went, all of the most bravest of us, we went out into the forest to battle the giants," he lifted his chin proudly, although his mother couldn't see because she was driving, "I was the leader of the most bravest warriors," he exclaimed, his childish voice ringing with pride.

"Oh, and did you and your *most bravest* soldiers find the giants?" his mother asked, playing along with his heroic tale. She smiled knowingly as he continued to ramble on about the giants and sea serpents. Occasionally throughout the story she hummed reassuringly at him to let him know she was still listening attentively and, if she didn't, her absence of voice was quickly persecuted with a loud "Mom! Are you listening?!" in which she would reply yes to and the grand story would continue with sudden pauses where he was thinking of what to say next. She tried to contain her laughter when he back tracked his story and when she asked him questions about it and the answer was far more elaborate than what she remembered the original story line being.

The boy, now a man, remembered these stories as he was led into the courtroom in handcuffs, his orange jumpsuit reflecting in the eyes of the audience as if this moment was no different than the rest of his life. It didn't seem to cross their minds that this... this was a mistake! The words cried out in his head, but no one could hear them; not even his mother. In court, there are no tales of sea monsters, there are no brave soldiers against the forest giants who had stolen his math homework in third grade. There is only the unsolved case of the woman who had been murdered a year ago; her body recently found in a ditch. He did not sit in the formidable chair of the judge, nor did he sit where the attentive attorneys perched like falcons behind desks of notes both written and typed. Nor was he one of the twelve jurors who sat next to him on his left. He was stationed between the wide-eyed panel and his criminal defense attorney, Adam Bird.

Mr. Bird was there not because he had to be, but rather because he wanted to be. He genuinely believed that Miller was innocent. After all, why would Miller, the accused, have killed a random woman? The thought haunted him as he looked to his left, eyeing the young man of twenty-three years. He was too young, Bird thought, too young to be dragged into this legal squabble between alibis, witnesses, court dates... For a moment, he was swept from his attorney's mask and the court room before him melted away under his pity for the younger man, but he quickly regained his stance. He could not allow such emotion to come in at a time like this. A time when Miller depended on him to do his job.

Adam could remember when he was a boy. He had told similar stories to his mother just as Miller had. Except his mother would not accept his fantasized vision of the world and sent him away to a boarding school. There, he lived until he graduated from college. He stayed at college and did not go home for the holidays. He even chose to continue his schooling without a summer vacation. He graduated three years ahead of his class. He was a smart man; graduating law school also at the top of his class.

However, separation at such a young age did something strange to his mind. Although the emotional division from his family was a choice in which he alone made, he would stay in his room feeling the weight of the world and his own emotions from his loneliness. Alone in his room because his friends had gone home to see their proud families and sit beside the glowing fire telling them of their studies, he sat accompanied by only the occasional glow of headlights streaming through the otherwise dark window. Slowly, his sanity ebbed away as if the overwhelming maw of his short childhood had opened a black hole and was sucking away at his life. That's when he decided to become a lawyer, more specifically a criminal defense lawyer, hoping it would resurrect his childhood. Yet, he didn't really know why, or how this would happen.

He felt a nudge from a boney elbow on his left that caught his attention. "Mr. Bird," the judge repeated, "would you like to make a closing on behalf of your client?"

Everything had gone as planned until this moment. Attorney Bird made the prosecuting attorney look like an idiot and made the witnesses look as though they were not even worthy of the butt in which they sat on in their chairs. He said what he wanted to say and regretted nothing. Lastly, he had achieved mastering his arguments without his speech impediment surfacing. It was a stutter that only seemed to take place when he was in court. But his stutter was caused by himself choking down impulsive lies and truths in which he notoriously gave out on a daily basis. The judge knew Adam Bird personally and knew of his stutter in court (although he did not know the truth about why he stuttered) and waited patiently as Mr. Bird stood up to begin his closing statement but began to trip over his words. Miller knew this as well, having learned about Mr. Bird because of his fame and appeal to the public.

Quickly, Bird scribbled down on a slip of paper what he didn't want to say out loud. It tricked his brain into thinking it had said something without the thought having an actual voice. He un-jammed his tongue from the back of his throat where it had caught his words, and he began his closing statement.

He's arguments are incredible, the judge thought very informally to himself as the attorney calmly summarized his evidence again but with a fresh spin so as to not be repeating himself and to appeal to the jury. *The jury would be crazy to find him guilty,* the judge's conscious whispered.

Miller straightened in his chair as his lawyer sat down in conclusion of his speech; it was the first time all day he had felt better about his odds of not going to prison. There was nothing more in the world the Miller wanted than not to go to prison for something he had not done. As Mr. Bird had rightfully defended: he hadn't even been in the state of Ohio where and when the girl was killed. Bird looked at his client with hopeful eyes; so caught up in his own self pride that he forgot about the note he had written that was now no longer on his table.

The jury then went to their special room and before Bird had time to get another cup of coffee, court was called back to order. The verdict was announced, and Miller Valaar was declared not guilty. Outside the court, Miller's mother came to him with tears in her eyes as he embraced her and his older sister, Mary. He shook hands with Adam Bird; the hands that had written the note and stolen it met for a final time.

Once home, Miller unlocked his apartment door and traveled straight to his couch. Its softness was welcoming after his long and stressful ordeal. He sat for a moment in the silence, his eyes gazing with no great intent at the parrot wallpaper. He then remembered the note and his hand drifted to his coat pocket. He retrieved the note and unfolded it. He then opened it and read to himself what it said: I killed the girl.

Character Sketch: Missing

I suppose everyone is a little bit different... some more than others. I tried to fit in – I promise you – but the road kept winding into a spiral and my once straight forward positive-thinking path soon became a labyrinth which forced me to go back all those miles I had come. As I grew up, more and more people surrounded me like padding in a football uniform. They made me look better, bigger, more protected than what and who

I actually was. In truth, the more "friends" I had, the lonelier I became. Imagine being isolated by a wall of your own friends. That's why I had to do it… to run away.

"And still missing is the 20-year-old student from Ohio. Allen Titan attended Ohio University until a year and a half ago today. He was last seen by his teammates in the varsity football locker room after practice." The T.V. above him buzzed.

"Allen has a slightly bulky structure standing at 6'1'', dark brown hair, and has a stationary artificial eye the right side. If you have seen Allen or heard from him, his family asks that you contact the local authorities for his whereabouts or any other information."

I sighed, bagging chips for the old man who had been a regular in the local store in upstate New York since he was my's age. Following the slow but steady man out to his car in the parking lot, I pushed the grocery cart while thinking about my life choices. One and a half years ago today I left my old life behind for something new. I hated being around the same boring people all the time. I wanted something fresh, I wanted to live and do what I wanted and not follow anyone else's schedule but my own. There should be no time in life other than working. True, I worked hard as a member of the football team those years ago and also my four years in high school, but there was nothing to learn from the college experiences I had, or my peers who were going to college for the same reason – so they must not know more than I do. No, experience is out doing what I am doing now. I didn't want to be working toward something with a large end goal in sight.

"Doing anything this weekend?" the old man inquired, leaning with huff against the old silver mustang.

"Working… also cleaning my apartment."

"Sounds pretty boring if you ask me. When I was your age, I was out having fun with my friends not worrying about cleaning and working. I didn't start working my first major job until my junior year when I got an internship. Say, where did you go to college anyway?" the man asked.

"Penn State," I lied.

"Oh, you must be quite the scholar," the man continued, "I was always a little more right-brained, a little more creative… not saying that you're not creative but you sound much more scheduled and organized than I ever was. Anyways, I usually considered everything *but* work and cleaning a big priority. Family also, I visited them during every holiday and the chances in between. Say, are you close with your family?"

"No," I replied.

"Gee, that's a shame," the old man frowned, "it's like you're missing half the picture."

"But work and making something of yourself in the world is what's important to me." I had finished unloading the bags by now, and was only staying to defend myself. "That's what matters in life. Everything else is just in the background."

"Believe what you like, but I think you need to reexamine your priorities. I always believed who you are and what you do whether it's at work or a family holiday party is what is important. It's not like they're going to bury you with your net worth stamped on your forehead."

As the old man drove off, I stood outside the store leaning against the cart feeling sympathy for the old man. I just wish he could understand the true meaning of life.

The Last Plant

Suelta Nateure felt the pressure increase in the greenhouse. Sweat dripped from her forehead, and her temples ached from stress and concentration. The heightened security didn't make her nervous, although she thought it was unnecessary because of the remote location. It was a difficult place to find especially through all the snow and mountains. Sometimes she felt trapped from the rest of the world, with only her years of research and training for this one plant to accompany her.

It was cold outside; the Colorado winter winds raked up and down the building, and she could hear the hum of the fans only because she stood near them. She straightened her back in discomfort, the time spent hunched over the table day after day beginning to take its toll on her vertebrae. She held an emerald green seed in her palm, examining its every groove and documenting its structure.

It was early morning, just after midnight, and what was thought would be the last liferoot plant had given this single seed. The scientists in training had gathered around earlier, before the plant had produced the seed she now tended to.

"It was only a tradition," they said while laughing nervously; but it was sad that after a few more years the tradition of honoring the liferoot might not continue. Not long ago, there were thousands of liferoot plants native to all parts of the world. There were so many, in fact, people used them in cooking and even for bathing and cleaning. The plants were used for virtually everything. As the years passed, the liferoot plant had become less and less abundant and more and more of a specialty item. In the last two hundred years, only a dozen had survived in several areas of the world. The plants were found, collected, and shipped in special blue pots to be housed in designated greenhouses throughout the world. Now, only a single plant and a seed survived here within the breathing walls of the green house.

It had been all over the news when the last one in Australia had died. Women wore black dresses and men were in suits and ties, all standing in the rain as cameramen with big umbrellas cast shadows on a world whose clock ticked in deafening silence. Every second could be the end.

Or not.

They are only whispers, Suelta reminded herself while putting the seed under a super powered lens. And most whispers in the world are not true. It was only a silly myth.

When there were only ten left three years ago, she was invited to a conference in Maryland.

"It's only a stupid superstition," she could hear the voice of the drunken man with the long brown beard tell her, "the survival of mankind," he laughed, "did not – *could not* – depend on the survival of the liferoot plant."

She squinted at the little speck before her, remembering that some people believed she held last ties to life in her hand. Slowly, she reached across the table and slid the blue pot filled of fresh soil toward her. She looked long into the dark brown soil, feeling the earth stare back and into her mind and soul. She then picked the seed from the dish and placed it firmly into the soil. It was heavy and sunk through the dirt easily.

Four minutes ticked by. Then fifteen. Then an hour. *Tick*, the clock cried, *tock*, it echoed. She sat in the chair, too tired to fall asleep. Three hours. Then four. As the hand reached the sixth hour, a small green stem reached through the soil and drank the air for the first time. She jumped upon seeing it shoot through so quickly, and watched as the stem grew up, up into the air. Leaves began to unfurl before her eyes as she watched life itself course through the plant and its leaves straighten. It reached out with its vines like arms reaching toward the sky and outward toward the horizon, making the plant tall and wide. It stopped finally when it reached about two feet all around.

Suelta steadied herself in her chair, taking in the feat she had just witnessed. Slowly, she got up, and touched the plant. It quivered beneath her touch, the leaves bouncing in the air. She admired it for only seconds longer, and then began tending to it.

Special plants require special treatments.

She first packed the soil's top layer with blue rocks. They were the same material the pot was crafted from and were said to promote growth and longevity. It was a product of modern science that she had yet to fully understand. Suelta then took a jar of clear paste from her cart and gently, carefully, began painting the stem of the plant. While she worked, her mind drifted back to the people outside the walls of the greenhouse. The people who counted on her for survival.

Or not.

It could only be a story.

It was mindless tasks of repetitious movements that always allowed her mind to wander. The people would never know if this plant supported their very existence until it was too late. She thought of all the places mankind would never go if this plant were to die, and all the places she would never know existed. What will happen if this plant does not produce a seed? If this is the last liferoot to ever live? How can that be fair if there are so many of us now, but only one plant? She thought of the small population of humans when the plants were so abundant compared to the small number of plants that existed now when humans were so abundant.

She had the ability to find out the answer now if she wanted to. The liferoot plant that produced this seed had grown terribly sick, and probably already died by now. It would be like ripping a band aid off a wound. No, she thought, I will not.

Hours passed and the sun had already warmed the top of the greenhouse and the plant had grown another foot taller and wider. Its emerald green leaves splaying out to catch the warm drops of sun. She had watered it once, the powerful liquid seeping through the mystical blue rocks and into the rich soil. The stems were strong already from the clear paste applied to the trunk, and the new shoots were absorbing the paste quickly. The pot was large enough to hold the plant for the entirety of its life. There were too many risks in replanting it, as this had unfortunately been proven many times before. Her steady hands were tired, but she kept tending to the plant, helping its thick base by moving the rocks around in the pot to accommodate its rapid growth.

No amount of scientific research could have predicted how long life on this planet would have lasted. It could have gone on until the dying lungs of Mother Earth heaved her last breath, or until a natural disaster decimated the human race. But human life was extinguished by mistake. Human fault alone can be blamed, for in a split second, her hand slipped, hitting the base of the plant. Darkness flooded all around as the gut-wrenching crack echoed in Suelta's ears, mind, and body as the roots ripped upward from their container, snapping flinging dirt onto the table and floor. No amount of blue rocks or scientific containers could have saved the fated liferoot plant. It hit the tabletop with a deafening pound, like a human heart's last drumming beat, and all that was became no more.

Author's Note:

The Last Plant is the first short story I published. It was featured in my college's literary magazine in the fall of 2016. This was my first year of college, and I was so excited to be published. Since then, I have had several other stories published in the same literary magazine, and each time I can honestly say that I feel the same joy as I did in 2016 when The Last Plant *was accepted. This story, in a slightly shorter form, also got an Honorable Mention in the 44th New Millennium Writing Awards.*

I feel so honored to have such supportive friend and family when it comes to writing and publishing. Friends who have come to readings I participated in at school, family who read my stories and even help edit.

This story captures my love of plants, and their importance in our lives. The Last Plant *tries to emphasize this importance through a dystopian-*

like Earth where one plant's life in particular seems to be tied directly to our own. When it dies, so do we. The people in this fictional society have lived so long with the plant around that no one knows for sure whether their lives are tied to this plant, and, of course, no one would know for sure until it is too late. They have taken for granted its life-giving qualities and for that they pay dearly.

Some of my stories, such as The Darkest Places of the Earth, *and this story, capture the importance of the environment and factors outside of humanity. Unlike* The Darkest Places of the Earth, *this story is about the direct tie between humans and their environment, where the other piece is more from an animal's perspective. On a different note, this piece also reflects on how science and all our technological advancements can seemly be meaningless in the face of human error.*

More Than a $20 Memory

===

Inspired by: Paint me a Birmingham by Tracy Lawrence

I stumbled to the edge of the railing, looking out over the Atlantic Ocean. Seven years ago, I lost my favorite hat here. Right on the pier with Lacy. Two years later we came back to the same spot, I proposed to her, and we got married that summer.

She loved that hat. Said it sat just right over my eyes, said it was like I could see right through her when I tilted my head. I'd like to think I could. I'd like to think I could have seen that far into her eyes.

The waves crashed against the rocks, and the sun seemed to melt into the distant white caps like butter. The wind gusted up, ruffling my hair, and I could feel the salt from the ocean lick at my feet.

I watched as the painter in front of me moved his brush onto the waves rolling back and forth along the sand on has canvas. He was an older gentleman, sitting in a small folding chair facing outward into the water, a bright yellow sunrise not yet dry painted onto the canvas in front of him. His short greying hair dripped sweat onto his thin shoulders, the sun almost reflecting off his dark skin. Each stroke of blue seemed to bring the ocean to life.

"Do you only paint ocean scenes?" I asked after a while, motioning to the canvas.

The man turned and smiled, "no, sir. For twenty dollars," he paused and shrugged his shoulders, "I'll paint you anything."

I looked down and saw a tin can with a slit in the top. Reaching into my pocket, I pulled out a ragged bill and slipped it into the can.

The old man took out a new canvas to replace the sunrise painting.

"Now, what can I paint you?" he asked.

"Could you paint me a small house, on the edge of a town. The house had a porch going all the way around up top, and a wooden swing to the left of the front door. And… there were daisies all along the front, with a long driveway and a yellow tin mailbox at the end."

He looked at me, his deep, kind eyes studied my face for a moment, and then he nodded with a smile.

"And my wife… put her on the porch swing. In her favorite blue dress."

He nodded again, "I'll have this done in forty-five minutes or so. If you'd like to get some breakfast, I'm a man of my word. I'll be right here painting, sir."

"If you don't mind, I rather enjoy watching you paint," I said.

He grinned, took out a clean brush, and began.

We were silent for a long time. I watched as he painted the grass, the house, and the flowers, before he spoke again.

"What did she look like?" his quiet voice seemed to come out of the ocean wind.

"My wife?"

"Yes, sir. Blond? Burnette? Red-head?"

"She was blond," I replied after a moment.

He fell silent.

"If you don't mind me asking, what happened to her?"

"God wanted her back," I said.

"How long were you married for?"

"Only three years," I replied softly.

"I've had two wives," he said after a moment. "The first one left me for a rich doctor. The second one passed away yesterday morning in her sleep."

"I'm… I'm very sorry to hear that," I said.

"She was a good woman. Always did the right thing, even when no one else would."

"How long were you married?"

"Twenty-three years," he replied.

"That seems like a lifetime."

The old man shrugged again.

Silence passed between us again, and I could hear only the murmur of the waves as they continued to clash against the concrete of the pier. Sea gulls cried over-head, and occasionally a fish jumped from the water and back down again into the blue.

He set down his brush and took the canvas down to dry. He took up his previous painting again, but by now the sunrise was long gone.

People stopped and looked, and a man in a business suit walked by and handed him two twenties, shook his hand, and took the ocean scene with him.

The old man sat back in his chair, looking over the pier.

"Son, your painting should be dry enough now. Just be careful with it."

"Thank you," I said, getting up. Lifting it cautiously, I held it up close to my face. It looked just like the house we had. "This is beautiful, thank you!"

He waved a hand dismissingly, still looking out on the ocean. I studied the painting once more, and then headed home.

In the evening sun, I hammered a nail up on the wall, and then wired the canvas. Upon hanging it, I stepped back to admire the scene from long ago. Lacy looked just like that, sitting on the swing, and the house was the same color white. Then, stepping closer, I squinted at the details, thinking my eyes were playing tricks on me. To my surprise, glowing light-yellow wings now came from either side of her. I shook my head, trying to clear my sight, blinked, and then they were gone.

Path of the Unforgotten

Everyone has a job or a destiny or a calling – the fact that mine involves dragging a body through the forest should be irrelevant.

The sky was clear, and the stars were starting to show themselves in the darkened sky. I shifted the rope from my right shoulder to my left and tugged as the bundle caught on a root. In an old forest like this one, it's nearly impossible to drag anything through here without it getting caught, bumped, and sometimes torn. But this time I had double bagged it, because last time when the bag tore, well, let's just say I'd rather not have to deal with that ever again.

The familiar sounds of the wolves howling crept into my conscious, and I quickened my pace. I had to deliver the body before they decided to come and investigate the trail I've left through the underbrush. Not this time.

The blue ribbon hanging from the loblolly pine ahead steered me left, and the path then followed a straight shot through. An owl up above *whooed* long and low, followed by the even chattering of the 'coons in the hollowed trees, and sound of the other damned nocturnal creatures scurrying through the fallen branches and dead pine needles. When the symphony of the forest reached the peak of its crescendo, all at once it grew quiet.

I stopped.

Not even a mouse so much as moved its little toe. In the silence, even an owl's soundless wings could have been heard. A deep *thrum* came from below my feet, quiet at first, breaking the deafening silence, but gathered in sound and volume as it shook the ground. Needles poured from above, littering my travel cloak and the bundle behind me, threatening to cover us and claim us as part of the forest floor – as many people had been. But it was the first test of the Carriers.

I whistled shrilly, and the shaking slowed and then all fell quiet again. The wolves howling started up once more and it urged my feet into action. One before the other, I hunched my back and felt the rope digging into my shoulder. It hardly felt anything like I remembered pain feeling when I was alive. That was a long time ago.

I could hear the stream ahead now, the icy waters like a fly trap for those who did not belong.

This was the second test.

The water enveloped my boot and the clearness of it was always startling. I tugged the bundle and it tipped down the bank headfirst into the bottom of the stream.

The body dragged across the stones and up over the berm on the other side, dirt collecting around where the water had touched it. I hardly noticed yet another blue ribbon guiding me forward back onto the pathway.

Nearly there, and only one more test to go.

I could start to see the city line visible through the trees, the lights of the kingdom danced and bobbed in and out between the trunks as I sauntered closer to the forest's edge. Today's was a special delivery, and this meant a large reward for me.

Finally, before me stood the old stone archway. Moss and lichen clung around its edges, and I would have been able to feel the heat from the clear, colorless flame if I could still push air through my lungs. The final test of innocence – only those wrongly put to death could pass through and be given to their receiver. Which is how I became a carrier; no one had come back for me.

I went through the archway with ease, hoping that the princess behind me could do the same. The bundle dragged through with no problem and so I continued on. The edge was just around the corner and I could see the prince standing with his arms folded across his chest. His pale face marked that of a boy who was not ready to see the forest between the realm of the living and the dead. He noticed me as I came closer, and relief crossed his face.

Vision of the Void

A crow flew overhead carrying a long shiny ribbon in its beak. Below it, a forest stretched on, unbreakable save the bog in the middle of it, and that's where the crow was headed.

The water was thick with lily pads in full bloom, their white flowers dotted between the impenetrable green like snow patches on the tops of otherwise barren mountains. Algae and duck weed speckled the top of the water. Even if a curious traveler were to make their way through the forest and happen upon this pond, they wouldn't be able to see to the bottom with all the greenery.

The crow landed on a fallen log that stuck out over the pond. He turned his head this way and that, looking at the bugs scurrying along the rotting bark. He gently laid the ribbon behind him, and then began inflicting mayhem upon the insects.

"What did I tell you about stealing my stuff!" a voice yelled from behind him.

He jumped, and emitted a small *squa* in surprise, wheeling around to see his assailant. "Well—"

"No, *well's*, *but's*, or any other excuses! I'm done with you taking my stuff, Jeromy!" she spat, snatching the ribbon off the log. "Why don't you go steal *useful* shiny things like money or something."

"Killian, we both know that's against the law," he chided.

"Crow's can't be punished under the law here, silly. You have to be a person."

"But I am a person!"

"The U.S. government doesn't think so," Killian sighed, sitting next to her friend on the log.

"Why did we even bother coming here?" the crow said, exasperated.

"I told you, we have to find her. I know she's here."

"You've been looking for this girl for months now, I don't think she lives here. I think we went through the wrong portal. *Maybe* she lives somewhere crows are considered to be people," Jeromy added.

"She's here. We just have to keep looking."

"Whatever," Jeromy said, going back to eating the insects.

She pushed back the long hair from her face and looked out into the forest line. Killian wished that the girl would just appear before her right then, and her search would be over and she could go back. But it wasn't so easy.

"What did you say this place was called?"

"Illinois," Killian replied distantly, still caught in her thoughts.

"Why Illinois?" Jeromy prodded.

"It's where the magic started. I told you all this before, but your bird brain just doesn't retain information." Killian looked over at Jeromy, frustration lining her brow.

He opened his beak to reply, thought better of it, and closed it again.

"Sorry, I'm just tired and hungry," she said, the softness Jeromy was familiar with returning to her eyes.

"Perhaps I can look again. She wears a shiny silver necklace, and lives in a grey and white house. She also has a black and white cat named Oreo," Jeromy recited.

"That's the one," Killian smiled.

"I'll be back," he said, taking flight.

"Watch out for the cat!" Killian called after him.

Jeromy flew up and over the forest again, and towards the city. It was only a few minutes time before he was circling around the buildings, eateries, and cars that filled the landscape. Though, he didn't quite understand how a girl who possessed no magic of the hand could help. What good was she? He landed in a low hanging branch and looked out onto the street below.

"I don't understand this place," Jeromy muttered to himself.

"Me neither," someone said from behind him.

He turned slowly to see a girl standing on the sidewalk, looking at him in awe.

"Was that you? That talked? A *bird*?" she said, frozen in place.

"I'm technically a crow, but—wait, how can you understand me?"

"I don't know," she breathed.

Jeromy flew out to the end of the branch, coming face to face with the girl. He looked her up and down. She had scuffed up shoes and paint splattered on one leg of her jeans. She had a backpack slung over one of her shoulders and her hair was thrown up carelessly.

"You're a sight for sore eyes. I thought you'd be fancier or something," he commented bluntly.

"Excuse me? How do you know me, who are you? How can a bird talk?"

"A crow," he corrected her again.

"Whatever," she exclaimed.

"Your name is Jane, right?"

"You're crazy. I'm going crazy," she said, walking away swiftly.

"Now, wait a minute," Jeromy chirped, flapping after her. "Your name is Jane, right?"

"Does it matter?" she snapped, still walking away.

"Yes, it does! Jane, my friend Killian and I need you! More than just us need you, actually," he continued.

"Go away, crazy bird," she said, turning up a driveway.

"How ridiculous! You're being called upon to fulfill your destiny and you're just walking away—" the front door slammed in his face.

He perched on the step outside the door. He could see into the house, and the flooring had holes in some parts and part of the step was missing on the first stair leading up beyond what he could see.

"I think you have me confused with another Jane. There are a lot of Janes here," a muffled voice said.

Jeromy skipped closer to the screen door and saw her sitting next to it, leaning against the wall.

"I don't think there are any other Janes that can hear me."

"Why are you here," she said softly.

"Do you remember when you were little, and you told everyone else that there was something special about the bottom of the pond in the middle of the forest just outside of town?" he asked.

"You mean when I was in grade school? How do you know about that stuff?"

"I haven't a clue what grade school is, but it was when you were little. You used to take your friends there and tell them, and they didn't believe you."

"It was just a stupid story. I just wanted to believe in somewhere other than here," she replied.

Jeromy was silent for a moment.

"Do you still have that silver necklace?" he asked.

"What? That super old ugly necklace? With the big silver disk on it?" she asked, giving him a side-glance.

"Yes."

"Yeah, but—watch out!!" she exclaimed, leaping to her feet.

Jeromy turned his head just in time to catch a blur of black and white was racing towards him. He bolted from the ground, but not before the cat snagged a feather from his tail with her claw.

Jane opened the screen door in desperation, and Jeromy darted inside. The door slammed behind, separating the huntress from her prey.

"Shoo, Oreo!" Jane scolded.

The cat in turn puffed herself up, arching her back to twice her size, and flattened her ears. Jane shut the solid door then, and all Jeromy could hear was a menacing *mew* from the porch.

"Sorry," Jane apologized. "Are you okay?"

"Only a feather gone," he reassured her.

"Only that and nothing more?" Jane mocked.

"It's 'only *this* and nothing more,' and I'm not a raven," Jeromy squawked.

"It was only a joke," Jane said, raising her eyebrows.

"May I see the necklace?" he said, ignoring her comment.

"Sure, as long as you don't poop all over my house."

"I'm not uncivilized," he replied with a small sigh.

She started up the stairs, and Jeromy flew up after her. At the top, she went left and then turned right into a small room. A neatly made bed with plain white linens sat pushed up against the wall, and a small wood dresser sat next to it. She opened the top drawer and pulled out a silver necklace with a circular metal plate hanging from the chain.

"What's so special about it?" she asked, laying it out on the bed.

Jeromy hopped up onto the comforter and pecked in the middle of the disk.

"Hey!" Jane exclaimed, but then fell silent as the necklace began to morph before her eyes until a key hung where the metal plate once was.

"Now do you believe me?" Jeromy asked, looking up at her.

"This was my mother's," Jane replied. "Did she know that it was a key?"

"I don't know the answer to that, but I know someone who might."

"Does it unlock the portal at the bottom of the pond?!" she asked excitedly.

"No, portals don't have keys, silly. Wait," Jeromy caught himself, "how do you know about the portal?"

"You just told me about it."

"No... I didn't."

"Oh."

Both sat in silence for a moment, looking at each other.

"Um, I don't know. That's what I always imagined was at the bottom. A portal to somewhere that just... wasn't here. That's all," Jane said quietly.

"Will you come with me?" Jeromy inquired.

"Where? To the pond?"

"You're smarter than you look," he replied. He picked up the necklace in his beak and took off down the stairs.

"Hey! That's my necklace!" Jane shouted after him.

"You're just going to have to follow me then, aren't you?" he shouted back in a muffled tone.

Jane ran down the stairs and out the front door, not even bothering to lock it behind her. She took off down the street, following the crow with the shiny chain tightly clenched in his beak. People looked at her as she ran past the houses, the traffic light on the corner, and the small shops and bakeries as she headed towards the forest. The road ended abruptly where a trail began, and she ran past a woman with a dog, a man on a bike, and several walkers as she continued farther and farther into the forest.

"Wait up!" she shouted. An elderly couple turned their heads in confusion. But she kept running, and soon she came to the deer trail she knew lead to the pond. Twigs snagged at her clothing and face, and briars tore at her pant legs. Her socks picked up burrs and hitchhikers as she made her way along the narrow trail. Finally, she came to the edge of the pond.

Cattails taller than herself lined around the edge of the water and spotted here and there between the forest line and the steep muddy bank. She looked up and saw the crow circling high above, like a vulture, or the sign of some foreboding prophecy. She hoped that she had not made a grave mistake in following her curiosity. She wondered if she were having an allergic reaction to something and all of this was a hallucination. Maybe she was dreaming? A part of her hoped that she wasn't.

"Hello?" Jane called out into the clearing. "God, I've gone nuts. I've really gone nuts this time," she muttered.

"You're not crazy," a voice from beside her said.

She jumped in surprise, nearly tripping on the mud and weeds into the pond. Beside her a woman sat on a log jutting out over the pond. The woman was older than her, but not terribly older. Her hair was long and unkept, and she had on a brown robe. The woman rose and came over to her.

"Who are you?"

"My name is Killian, and you must be Jane," she said, a glowing smile across her face.

"Yes, I am. How—? You know what, I'm just going to stop asking questions. Can you tell your crow to give me back my necklace?" she asked, irritation creeping into her voice.

"Oh, my apologies. Jeromy!" the woman called.

The crow descended with a graceful swoop and landed on Killian's shoulder. He then dropped the necklace into her outstretched hand. Killian held the key up in front of her, inspecting it. It was oddly smooth, and the rounded handle showed no sign of imperfection in craftsmanship or age. She unclasped the chain and fashioned it around Jane's neck. It was lighter than Jane remembered, but it had been years since she had worn it.

"You hold the key to our survival, and the time has come for you to use it," Killian finally said.

"I don't understand," Jane replied. "What does it do?"

"When Earth became more populated by the human race, a war emerged between two sides. One side possessed magic of the hand, and the other a magic of the mind. In the end, the users of physical magic decided to separate themselves from the other humans and built a separate realm away. But as time has gone on, your kind have forgotten your abilities," Killian explained.

"What do you mean, *magic of the mind*?" Jane asked.

"I believe your modern society has come to coin it: *the imagination*, or something of the likes. The ability to create an idea that has no tangible body within the physical realm but can exist in the minds of others through words, drawings, and other mediums. But, over time it has lost its power in your realm both in creation and in practice. Now it is time to restore it back. The two realms will be balanced once more, but it's up to you to release it back into your world. Your pent-up magic has returned to my realm – unused and raw. You see, it must go somewhere if it's not being used here," Killian clarified, gesturing around her. "It is dangerous for one realm to possess them both at once, as history has told us."

Jane looked across the pond. The blue sky was clear, and the bright green leaves of the forest beyond waved gently in the breeze. She wondered what she should do. She still had so many questions she didn't know the answer to.

"How?" Jane asked, her curiosity running wild.

"Beyond the portal, there is a box in which the key belongs to where your realm's magic is held. All you have to do is open the box. It's up to you."

Jane looked down at the key around her neck. It glinted in the sunlight as the breeze twisted it this way and that.

"So, what are you going to do?" Jeromy asked.

Somewhere above, another crow cawed. She wondered if it, too, had an interesting story to tell.

Minisaga: The Tree

Leaves sway in the wind as children play tag in the shade of her boughs. One child trips and falls to the Earth floor. The other children laugh and do not notice but the tree cradles him in her leafy fingers, knowing one day he will grow up.

Shady Vale

I

"It's nice, this assisted living complex," she had told Betty the first day they met. "It's got big windows, good food, and a constant fluctuation of new people."

She had a large room on the second floor, right across from Betty's, which is ultimately how they had met. This morning she woke up earlier than usual, the birds chirping loudly outside her window. She was quite sure by now that they had built a nest in the tree right by her window, as they had woken her up now the third time this week. She tried to roll over and get more sleep, still with forty-five minutes until eight o'clock, the usual time her and Betty ate breakfast together. She thought of the café on the fourth floor and wondered if there would be blueberry muffins this time. *God*, she thought, *I have to tell them about these damn birds.*

Soon she realized there was no more sleep to be had, so she got up, brushed her teeth, and dressed for the day. She made herself tea, something she had adapted to in the last five years after her husband, Frank, had passed away. He used to bring her tea every morning in her favorite china – the expensive kind.

She remembered it clearly, the red and white tea set. It was a crimson colored red, like blood.

Now all she had were coffee mugs with the words "Shady Vale" printed on the side and "*where you'll feel right at home!*" below in small italicized font.

She checked her watch, finished her tea, and then headed out the door. As usual, Betty was stepping out at the same time, and smiled brightly.

"Good morning, Maggie!" she cooed.

"Morning," she grumbled. "These bird's chirping woke me up early, I'm going to go tell the front desk today after breakfast so they can get rid of them."

"Oh, Maggs, you don't mean that! I would love it if I woke up to birds chirping outside my window every day!" she exclaimed, pushing the up arrow for the elevator.

"Well, good then! You can have 'em! I'll tell them to put the nest right in your room on your nightstand right next to your bed!" Maggie laughed bitterly.

"You don't mean it…" Betty repeated.

II

Diary,

Today I moved from my beautiful house to Shady Vale. I couldn't help but think of all the memories Frank and I had here, all these memories left in these walls and in these floors. If only there was a way to reverse time and change what had happened. If only he had ██████ ~~oner~~ so that I could have moved on with how I wanted to live my life. I love it when Frank would leave the house early in the morning for work, and I would have the day to myself. I wonder if he ever found out about ██████.

III

"I'll have a coffee, with extra creamer and sugar," Maggie commanded.

"Okay," the barista said, trying to still sound friendly. "Do you want whipped cream on it?"

"No, I don't want whipped cream! Do you want me to die an early death?!" she snapped.

The young woman hesitated, thinking better of herself, and then replied, "no ma'am."

"I'll get a hot chocolate, *with* whipped cream," Betty chimed, stepping up to the counter.

They found comfortable seating where they always did, near the back and at a circular booth. The green and ivory stripped walls seemed to melt into the ivory tile and the matching upholstery.

"When I was 19 years old, I used to come to a café that was just…"

"Yes, I know Betty, you told me this story last time. And the time before that. Your younger sister used to try to get boys from your class to talk to you, and she would always invite them to sit next to her," Maggie interrupted.

"You always have such a good memory, Maggs, and you're such a good listener. I couldn't have asked for a better friend,"

Maggie grunted.

"I wonder what ever happened to my dear little sister," Betty said.

"She died forty years ago from cancer," Maggie stated bluntly.

"Oh yeah, I remember now. That was the saddest funeral I've ever gone to. Not a single person there had dry eyes. Except my mother, who had cried so much already she told me she had no more tears in her left. Said she had used them all up."

"That's nice," Maggie replied, looking out the window.

IV

Diary,

Today I woke up and remembered Frank's funeral. It was yesterday, and God bless that he is fi~~██████~~. Now I can ~~have the bed to myself~~. But I miss how he always used to bring me tea, and breakfast in bed. Something he had always done since we were married, except the nights █
███████████████████████████████
██████. Work, you know, was quite busy in those days.

V

"Why didn't you get whipped cream in yours?" Betty asked, scooping her own with her straw and eating it.

"You're not supposed to put *whipped cream* on *coffee*, Betty," Maggie replied, "and I don't like it, anyway. Not on anything."

"Nothing at all?"

"Nope."

Betty was silent for a moment, her attention directed to the new people coming into the café, and then her eyes averted to the window, people with shorts and even dresses walked about below them.

"It looks like a nice day outside," she remarked.

"Mmmm."

Betty picked up the daily activities paper that was always laying on the table every morning in the café.

"It says that they are having outdoor activities today. They have butterfly watching outback, you know, by all those flowers. And they also have meditation on the lawn by those stones. You know where I'm talking about, Maggs? Remember those stones under those huge oak trees?"

"I can't do anything with you today, Betty," Maggie said after a moment.

"Well, why not?"

"Because I'm supposed to say in here," Maggie stirred her coffee.

"Why?"

"Because I need to be close to the hospital, if something happens."

"What are you talking about?" Betty insisted, concern flooding into her blue eyes.

"I went in for a check-up last weekend, and the doctors are concerned with my health," Maggie concluded.

"For God's sake, Maggs! What's wrong?" Betty nearly shouted.

"Forget it, Betty, you wouldn't understand. And you'll probably forget in a couple weeks, so I'll have to keep re-explaining it to you."

"No, you won't, Maggie. I wouldn't forget something like that. Just tell me what's the matter," Betty prodded again.

"Just forget about it."

VI

Diary,

Today, I decided I had waited long enough. Especially after ███████████. Frank was meant to ██████, his heart somehow holding on longer than I had ever thought it would. I would at least live the rest ██████████, ██████ ~~money~~ ██████████ ~~myself~~. If ████ ~~had to~~ ██, then Frank should have to, as well.

VII

Betty had long since finished her hot chocolate. She looked at Maggie and felt only confusion. Did she have this problem before? How long had she not been able to go outside? She swirled her straw around in her empty cup.

"I need to tell you something, Betty," Maggie said finally. "I need to get this off my chest."

"Is this about not being able to go outside?" Betty wondered aloud.

"Well... sort of. Can I tell you a story?"

"Of course," Betty pipped.

"I once knew someone, who wanted a lot of money. She believed that if she married someone rich, she would be happier. This rich man also had a heart condition, and he told her that he probably wouldn't live past his 30s. He asked her if she would still love him, even though that. She made him believe that she didn't care, that she would love him no matter what. And to an extent that was true... except that it did matter. She married him for this reason. And so, they lived happily, until one day she met someone else. A man she worked with. He was rich too, and had the same shrewd mind that she did. She told him everything, and they made a decision to marry after her husband died... but R— the other man, died unexpectedly, and she was left alone with her husband. She grew older, and older, and still her husband didn't die. She was filled with regret, anger, and sadness. The feeling of wasting her whole life away. And so, she did only what she thought she could."

Betty listened with intent that soon became shock. And then she sat back in her chair, numb to the world around her.

"Why are you telling me this, Maggie? Is that story true?" she asked, her voice only a whisper.

"You decide, but whatever you choose to do with the information, know that whoever you tell probably won't believe you. I'm sorry I have burdened you with this, but I realize now that having you as a friend wasn't an accident. I knew that if I told you this, no one would believe you. But instead I found only more regret, as I soon realized that you have become my only true friend throughout my life, and I have made many mistakes. And I know this now, after meeting you."

"I can't believe this... I'll... I'll tell someone!" Betty spat.

"They won't believe you."

"Why not!" she demanded.

"I think we both know why."

Betty got up abruptly and left, leaving the activities list behind.

VIII

Diary,

Today, R̶ ▇▇▇ died in a car crash. I got a call from the hospital. The woman said I was his emergency contact. I was in disbelief. ▇▇▇? ▇▇▇ who lives on 2nd Street? ▇▇▇ with a porch swing? ▇▇▇ who had an old green car, and a Model – T he had just bought at an auction across the country? *My* ▇▇▇? How could that be? I asked her how could that be? He was perfectly healthy yesterday. Only just in his 40s. Please tell me he isn't dead.

IX

Betty opened her door and looked across the hall. Maggie hadn't come out yet, but she would in a few moments, she thought. She waited. She checked her watch. Fifteen minutes ticked by and still no movement, not even a light emitted from under her door. Maybe she had already gone up.

She went to the elevator and hoped that while she was waiting Maggie would show up. When the door opened, she hoped for the same thing.

In the café, she searched the bathroom, noticed their empty table, and checked everyone who was in line. She went back down the elevator and stood before Maggie's room. She listened, cupping her hand like a child would to overhear a conversation through their parent's bedroom door.

"Maggie?" she called, knocking lightly on the white door. "Magg's, are you in there? It's time for breakfast!" she tried again.

Still nothing.

She tried the handle, and found it unlocked. Slowly, she opened the door, not wanting to startle Maggie if she were still in bed. The room was dark, the blinds still drawn, and the only source of light was the lamp on the desk across from the bed.

"Maggie!" Betty said, relieved. She walked swiftly over to her friend sitting at the desk, slumped over a tattered looking book. "Maggs, come on! Wake up, it's time for breakfast."

She shook her friend, but nothing happened.

"Maggie?" Betty whispered. The only sound in the room was her own breathing, and the faint chirping outside the window. "Maggie," she said again, fear beginning to creep into her voice.

"Maggie!" she screamed, frantically trying to find a solution. "Someone help!" she yelled again, sobbing now as she tried again to wake the pale body.

A man and a woman rushed into the room. The woman's yellow sweater reminded her of the daffodils outside her house. Home. Where was that? She hadn't visited her mother in a long time. Where…?

"Miss, please move aside. We can get her from here," the woman said calmly, taking Betty's arm and leading her away. Two more men came down the hall toward the room. The woman led Betty back to her own room and sat her down at the edge of the bed.

"What's your name, Miss?" the woman asked.

"Betty. Betty Overlock," she said between her increasing gasps and sobs.

"It's nice to meet you, Betty. My name is Nicole. I'm going to ask you to take some slow, deep breaths, and then when you are ready, can tell me what you know about Maggie?" she said calmly, taking Betty's hand to comfort her.

Betty looked at the floor, watching the tears slide from her face onto the carpet. She thought for a moment, not sure what to say. Finally, she lifted her head.

"Maggie and I have been having breakfast now for a few years together, and this morning she didn't come out from her room. I checked the café, the table we usually sat at, and even the bathrooms. So, I came back here and knocked on the door. She must have unlocked it when she got up, because I tried the handle and it opened. And she was just sitting there at her desk. And I tried to wake her up, but she wouldn't move. I'm… I'm so scared Nicole… is she going to be okay?"

The woman pursed her lips. "I'm not sure, Betty, but we will definitely be sure to pass any news onto you. For now, why don't you and I go have breakfast this morning, okay?"

Betty nodded slowly, whipping her face.

"Let me go get my purse, and I will be right back," she squeezed her hand with a smile, and then left the room. Betty sat in silence for a moment, and then looked at the door. Fear overtook her as she remembered the notes Maggie was hunched over. She jolted to her feet and almost ran across the hall. The door was still open, and the vacant room greeted her coldly. She made her way to the desk and took the book in her hands. The journal was turned to the middle, and she skimmed through the beginning of it. All that was left were entries with the incriminating evidence blacked out. Betty slipped the book into her purse and stepped out the door to wait for Nicole.

Essay: The Reclaiming of North America

Long before a human foot was ever placed onto the North American soil; birds, little furry bunnies, and woodland deer claimed this land as their own. Barn owls and bald eagles perched peacefully on the branches of trees that had not yet been cleared by the imperialistic Europeans. The harmless forest animals who witnessed the desolation of their homes will never forget what was done to them, nor will they forgive those who did it. In modern day times, it is assumed by most that deer, squirrels, and chipmunks – among others – are rather unintelligent, and the only instinct they possess is to survive. This assumption may be true, but these forest dwellers hold within their survival plans the unfettered desire to reclaim their continent – holding nothing back. These animals can be separated into three main groups: The Annoyance, The Risk Takers, and The Sly. Furthermore: the ones that succeed, and the ones that do not.

The Annoyance are the mice in the walls of your bedroom that wait until you go to bed and then scratch the walls for hours on end. These mice or other small animals know all the rooms in your house. They know when you are at home, what times you eat and, most importantly, where you sleep. If they are not in your bedroom annoying you when you are trying to go to sleep, they are either in your kitchen scratching or making nests in your attic and basement. Flying squirrels are most known for their ability to position themselves in your attic and/or basement. They rip out the insulation in your walls and build nests in any place that is the most inconvenient for you. If you find hordes of acorns in random places in your storage room, chances are you are being attacked by The Annoyance. Once the Annoyance has targeted you, there is no escape from their sadistic nature.

Another prime area to find The Annoyance is your own back yard. Some houses have decorative rock walls that are perfect for chipmunks to burrow into and make nests between. If enough chipmunks do this, a heavy rainstorm could washout the wall causing hundreds of dollars in repair. Moles tunnel through the middle of lush, grassy yards, driving dads from sea to shining sea into the ocean of madness – a maw of no escape and endless headache no Advil will cure. The "harmless" deer that ate literally *all* your vegetation planted that spring also belong to this group. The skunk that sprayed your dog the other day—a little gift signed, sincerely yours, The Annoyance.

Mostly everyone who is familiar with the concept of a car also knows the joke about animals that seem to wait for a driver to roll by until they make a mad dash for the other side. This is not a joke. Rather, it is a serious problem and a well-developed plan acted out by The Risk Takers. Perhaps the discovery of The Risk Takers will finally answer the infamous question of why the chicken crossed the road. This specific group of animals suffers the most fatalities and is open to all types of animals. The goal is to get the car to swerve in effort to not hit the cute, innocent animal. Do not be fooled. Humans have been seriously injured from hitting a tree in attempt to not hit the cute, fluffy bunny, and in serious cases fatalities have occurred. This is exactly what that sadistic bunny wanted. Beneath his pelt of fur and flesh resides a heart of ice and a brain buzzing with revenge and world domination. Often, these Risk Takers will die, but the lucky ones will live or come away with battle scars. Squirrels and raccoons with missing tails are most likely Risk Takers who barely escaped with their life.

The Sly are the plotters in the shadow, the glowing eyes in the night, the harbingers of death, and they live among us. They can be seen every day within the safety of the forest as you drive to work, school and home. They are the animals to be feared and above all respected. The Sly are an elite intelligence group superior to the other two and create the plans and evil schemes that are carried out by The Annoyance and The Risk

Takers. These animals are rarely close to the front lines and suffer little to no fatalities. While taking a nature walk in the heart of enemy territory, The Sly can be seen. They look as though they are doing nothing… maybe they are foraging for food or sitting on a log looking around or up in a tree sleeping. They may give you the false impression that they are the innocent animals and know nothing of war. No woodland animals are innocent—do not let them deceive you. They never sleep. They are always plotting against the humans of North America. They are the "man behind the curtain." They are the harbingers of chaos.

Within the merciless groups of The Sly, The Risk Takers, and The Annoyance, there are those who succeed and those who do not. Each group is different, and death is not necessarily a failure. For example, A Risk Taker who lost his life in the act becomes roadkill, which displeases most human beings because they do not want to look at the gruesome carcass in the road. In a way, this Risk Taker becomes part of The Annoyance by disrupting traffic and making humans uncomfortable. Since the ultimate goal of these animals is to reclaim North America in any way possible, those animals who contribute to this are the successful ones, and the ones who do not are considered unsuccessful.

With The Annoyance trying to drive humans insane and destroy their homes, The Risk Takers attempting to pick off humans one by one via running into the road, and The Sly working as the coordinator of these operations, North America is sure to fall into the impending doom constructed by woodland creatures. Most humans are unaware of this serious threat and if the dangerous gangs of animals inhabiting North America succeed to defeat us, they will surely strive for world domination. It is without a doubt a hairy situation that cannot be ignored. The great footprint of mankind upon the world threatens to be scoffed out by millions of little animal prints.

Fire

"Wow."

"What?" he asked.

"Just… wow…"

"Seriously, what?!"

Peony pointed to the forest below them, the trees like a giant green sheet of raw wilderness. "Just the whole of it… the vastness of it… it's just a lot to take in, that's all."

"Yeah well... that's why I took you here. I thought you would appreciate it. A lot more than the other people I've taken here," he commented.

"Who else?"

"Oh," Wyatt said, "well, for starters, I took my family here once and the whole time they were complaining about the hike up the mountain. Then, some old friends from high school and you know how that goes..."

She nodded slowly, not taking her eyes off the landscape.

"It's really amazing to me how much we take places like these for granted. I mean, even though its practically in our backyard, not everyone in the world lives in a place like this," he said after a moment. There was a small river below them that he was particularly fascinated with. He watched as the water moved along the rocks and logs slowly, as if the rest of eternity had its arms wide open in embrace at the ends of the earth for the small, liquid stream of dappled blues and greens.

"Maybe that's what makes it special," she replied.

The footsteps behind them nearly caused them both to fall right off the cliff in surprise, however, when two other hikers emerged, they caught their breath, looked at each other, then laughed.

The new hikers stood on the other side of the view holding hands and being sweet towards one another.

Peony turned towards Wyatt and rolled her eyes, motioning towards the path down. "Come on, let's go before we contract air-born cooties," she joked.

Unexpectedly, the boy hiker stepped back and got down on one knee, pulling out a ring from his fancy hiking backpack. The girl hiker squealed in delight, and instantly burst into tears.

"Wait," Wyatt said quietly, "what if I wanted to propose to you, too?" he smirked.

"Fat chance," Peony replied without skipping a beat, "besides, I feel like you definitely shouldn't after someone else did in the *exact* same spot. That's a *real* mood killer."

"Yeah… besides, I wouldn't want an engagement to be the *peak* of our relationship."

"That's not even a good one," she replied.

"Are any puns actually good? I feel like the whole point is for them to be absolutely God awful," he said.

"Good point," she laughed.

"So, what else do you want to do today?" Wyatt asked.

"Ugh… how much do you like ice cream? Because I could really go for some orange sorbet."

"Who doesn't like ice cream? Also, isn't sorbet different from ice cream?" he pondered.

"Yeah, I guess it is. But it's still really good," she stated firmly.

He looked at the ground as he descended the look-out point carefully. Root and large rocks protruded from the well-worn path, and he didn't want to slip or trip over one of them and make a fool of himself. Although he and Peony had known each other since middle school, he still didn't want to embarrass himself in front of her, especially now that they had a thing. At least, he thought they had a thing. He wasn't sure whether she also thought this, but from the standpoint of his over analytical mind, he was *sure* they had a thing. At the very least, he knew he liked her. She reminded him of fire, and he knew that fire was something his mother had always told him to stay away from.

"I'm not looking forward to this week. I have three tests I'm really worried about. I don't think Dr. Benson will let me take his test early, which would have been nice," she said, using a tree as support while she stepped over a fallen log.

"Dr. Benson is nice; you just have to give him time. It's early in the semester, and he's still trying to act all tough. He's hilarious; once he lightens up," Wyatt added.

"Dr. Benson assigns too much homework. How does he expect us to have a life outside of his class?"

"I'm not sure he does… but it gets better," he reassured her, "just trust me."

"I trust you, Wyatt," she said, turning her head and smiling back at him. "I just don't trust Dr. Benson. He also needs a wardrobe change."

Wyatt laughed, "yeah, that's what happens when you still think it's the 80's."

The sound of voices traveled around the corner, and soon Wyatt could see a group of girls from school coming up the path towards them.

"Oh, look at you two!" The blonde girl in front exclaimed, her orange tank top riding up more than what he thought was accidental. "Out on a date," she concluded, stopping and putting her hands on her hips.

"Oh, we're not dating," Peony countered quickly, not even letting a second of silence slip between their exchange.

"We're just friends," he interjected, hoping to ease the awkwardness with solidarity.

"OK, but when you two love birds hook up a month from now, I'll want to say, 'I told you so,'" she laughed, and the girls behind her giggled.

"I'm sorry Penny, but unlike you I don't participate in hook-up culture," Peony retorted, and then pushed past them. Wyatt hesitated before following without comment.

"Are you okay?" he said after they were out of earshot of the girls.

"Yeah, I'm just so tired of people assuming," she huffed.

"That's right; smash the patriarchy!!" he exclaimed. Peony shot him a look, her brown eyes piercing.

"Or not," he offered.

"I'm ready for some ice cream," she said, turning and continuing down the path.

His car wasn't far from the trail head, and soon they were driving back down the winding road towards town. He couldn't help but feel the sting of Peony's words *'we're not dating,'* and turned up the radio in hopes of drowning out the sound of his own thoughts.

***

The alarm clock next to his bed read 3AM, and he watched mindlessly as the green colons between the three and the zero pulsated on and off. It was approaching Valentine's day, and he couldn't get the stupid idea of asking her out from his head. His roommate rolled over in his sleep, kicking the stuffed animal panda bear off the bed in the process. The panda's butt, which seemed to be filled with ten thousand beads of plastic, made a loud *plop* noise as it hit the ground. *A stuffed animal, oh, that's genius.* He smiled wildly into the dark. *Thank you, panda butt,* he thought, and turned over and shut his eyes.

***

"Sorry, what?" Peony said, confusion and panic glistening in her eyes.

"Will you be my Valentine?" Wyatt said again, extending his arms and the stuffed pink and white "Love Panda" towards her.

"That's... really sweet," she said sincerely, but her brow furrowed in concern. She took the panda slowly.

"I'm being serious," he said, almost so quiet she couldn't hear. "I really mean it. And, I know this came out of nowhere, so whatever happens –

well, I hope something happens – but even if it doesn't, I guess… you know what I mean!" he muttered, hoping, praying.

"Wyatt, I… I don't really understand. Are you asking me out?" she asked, using the same quiet tone.

"Uh… only if you're going to say yes. But if you're going to say no, we can just pretend that this never happened," he answered in a rush.

"Wyatt, I'm sorry but… I just don't feel that way about you. I'm so sorry…" she said, looking at the ground between them.

"I'm sorry…"

"It's okay, I…"

"Do you want the panda back?"

"No! God, no. It was a gift to you. I'm not taking it back just because… just think of it as a gift from a friend. Happy Valentine's day, Peony."

"Happy Valentine's day to you, too."

***

"I don't really understand, are you asking me out?"

The words repeated in his head like a drum.

***

Graduation flew by, and before he could stop and think about all he had learned and all he had lived through, he was already being accepted into graduate school programs and planning for the future. Wyatt looked at the picture of Peony and himself holding the bouquet of flowers their parents had brought them. Hers were bright yellow sunflowers, and his were deep red roses. He smiled, picking the picture up from the desk. That picture was taken about two years after he had tried to ask her out. Eventually they had learned to laugh the whole thing off. He could never quite shake the event off as if it were nothing, just like she still had the pink and white panda.

Just like he was just one of her many friends. *Just friends*. He put the picture back on his desk and stared blankly at his computer.

***

"Peony? For God sake, what are you doing here?" he exclaimed, stopping in the middle of the sidewalk.

She rushed to hug him, and he held her tight.

"I just wanted to see where my best friend ended up in life. You know, doing research and grown up things at a graduate school," she replied cheerfully.

"You never cease to surprise," he said, stepping back with a smile.

"I've missed you so much! Are you busy right now, or can you catch up over a cup of coffee?"

"Actually, I just got done for the day. Come-on, I'll show you this really cool place downtown of the campus. I think you'll like it," he smiled.

He couldn't believe that she had really come all this way to visit him, and he couldn't stop smiling the whole way to the coffee shop.

"She's still running for ya, eh?" Peony smirked, patting the dashboard of the old car.

"Works like a charm," he replied, shutting off the engine.

"Wow, what a cute café! I love the big windows and wood accents," she remarked, looking out the window.

"The inside is even better," he said, stepping out of the car.

They ordered their drinks and sat at a small square table near the window overlooking the street. Wyatt fidgeted in the silence, pretending to look out the window as Peony seemed to do the same.

"How's veterinary school?" he finally asked.

"Eh, you know; animals," she joked, grinning at him.

"It's good to see some things haven't changed," he laughed.

The barista came and gave them their drinks, and Wyatt began to drown in the silence again.

"How's your famil—"

"I have something to—"

"You go first," Wyatt said.

She paused, her eyes looking down into her drink. "I have something to ask you," she said quietly.

"Okay."

"Do you remember sophomore year of undergrad, on Valentine's day…" she drifted off.

"Depends…" he said, averting her eyes and fidgeting with his coffee cup.

She sighed. "I'm sorry to bring this up, as awkward as it was… and is, I guess. But I really wanted to tell you that I can't stop thinking about how I reacted that day."

Wyatt unintentionally ripped the cardboard liner around his coffee cup off.

"And I can't help but think that maybe I was wrong. I think I just got nervous and... I can't believe I actually drove all the way up here to tell you this," she added under her breath. "I can't stop thinking about...you."

His hand paused; his fingers stopped trying to push back together the ripped ends of the liner. He looked up at her, the tension in his body holding his shoulders at a ridged angle.

"Peony..."

"No, it's okay if you don't feel like that anymore. I've just been holding that in for so long I needed to tell you. Maybe that wasn't fair to do, but I just had to settle it," she said hurriedly.

"Peony," he stated again. "I appreciate you telling me but... I've had a lot of time to think about it and, I just don't want to ruin this. This friendship… it means a lot to me…" He struggled for words.

"We had something, Wyatt. We had something and I ignored it, and now you want to go back to us just pretending we don't have something more going on between us? We have a whole world out there Wyatt, a whole world where we can do anything! A whole world to make our own adventure, and you don't want to talk about it? What are you afraid of?" she pressed.

"I just… I just think that we're so different now. You're going to vet school and I'm here doing research. We're not at the same school anymore and then you might find someone else who's smarter than me or interested in more of the same things as you and that makes you laugh more or takes you out to dinner more or invites you over more…"

"Stop!" she exclaimed. "Why would I care what other people are like when I'm here telling you that *I* like *you* for how you are? Heck, you're the guy that had the guts to buy me a panda for Valentine's day when you didn't know what I'd say. And even after I said no, you're still here as my friend. There has to be something in that."

"I'm sorry Peony… I just can't commit to something like this right now."

She turned her head to look out the window, trying to shield him from seeing the tears beginning to glisten in her eyes.

***

He pulled into the parking lot of her apartment and sat in his car for a long time. He wondered if anyone else was watching him just sit there. He wondered if someone was going to call the police on him. He wondered the alternative which was that no one saw him and that no one really cared. Both scenarios were startling to him. He shut off his car.

After a moment he opened the door and immediately the chill of the night seeped through his clothes. He pulled the jacket around himself tighter and pulled up the collar. He walked up the stairs to the second floor, and then stood in front of her door. He was thankful that it was cold out, or he didn't know how long it would have taken him to knock on her door. He waited a moment, and then knocked again. The doorknob turned and pulled inward, revealing behind her a small living room with a glass of what looked like whiskey sitting on the table next to the sofa.

"Wyatt," she gasped.

"Peony, I know this is crazy. And I know that you came to see me only two weeks ago… and I know that I just wanted to be friends, but I was wrong, and I regret it and I love you, and—"

She pulled him from the hallway and kissed him.

Warmth filled his body and he remembered again what fire was like when she put her arms around his neck: beautiful, passionate, and always dangerous.

The Darkest Places of the Earth

"The world is big and I want to have a good look at it before it gets dark" – John Muir

Between the smallest pine trees on the edge of the forest, a wolf sat, and waited. The moon was far above, and the light reflected off the dew coating the leaves and needles above him, and grass of the meadow before him.

The wolf's ears pricked as he heard the soft steps of the bear from behind him. The wolf did not move to greet the bear as she stood beside him. The unlikely pair sat in silence for a moment, listening to the night sounds.

"This darkness is unlike any other," the bear said softly.

The wolf said nothing.

"We will have to move again soon," the bear urged.

"Where will we go? We cannot keep moving from forest to forest. Eventually we will have to stay, and let our fate be determined for what it will," the wolf grunted.

"We have to keep fighting, if not for ourselves, but for those that have yet to see the forests of the world," the bear replied quickly.

But the wolf was old and tired, grey hair flecked through his coat, and scars marked his left flank from the troubles of the past. The bear was young, and she had many stories yet to tell.

"I am going to tell my sleuth to leave starting tomorrow morning, and we will go north looking for more forests. Maybe if we go deep enough into the wood, we will never be found there. You should tell your packs to join us at least and come along yourself if you will."

Again, the wolf said nothing.

"The deer have already begun to move, and many others, as well; soon there will nothing here for you."

"I will tell my packs to move along with you, but I am tired of running. I cannot go again. I fear that I will make it through another winter, and I would rather live in a land familiar to me than a foreign ground, foreign water, foreign sky and trees; I know this forest too well, and the only sunsets I want to see are from between these two trees."

"They will come for you by the end of this cycle."

"And I will be here to greet them."

The bear and the wolf looked out onto the meadow, and the barren space beyond it, the soil turned yellow and the trees all gone. There were large piles of dirt upheaved from the earth, and no life, save the occasional curious rabbit, wandered there.

"Old wolf, you have given up, but I will promise you that your pack will not. A new leader will be named, and they will travel north with us, and we will make a new home for ourselves."

The wolf sat in silence and listened as the bear went back into the pines. It was early morning now, and yet he still did not move. The birds had stopped chirping, and it was so quiet he could hear his breathing, and the beating in his own chest. He knew the light coming up over the horizon was not the sun, for he was facing west. They were the lights that made the forests disappear. And so, he closed his eyes, and he waited.

Acknowledgments:

Thank you to my family for supporting my writing and buying my books and asking questions and just everything. Thank you.

Thank you to my friends for also supporting me and following my writing adventures.

Thank you to my roommate, Kaitlin, for #1 living with me, and #2 taking wonderful pictures for my book release. And for everything else you do (I would list them here, but I fear the page count would drive up the printing cost).

And thank you Evan. For everything. Your encouragement, optimism, and advice. Thank you for all of it a thousand times over.

Last but not least: thank you reader! Without you, these stories would not live.

Made in the USA
Monee, IL
14 March 2021